The Mystery Monster

ALADDIN   New York   London   Toronto   Sydney   New Delhi

Paige
PROVES IT

BOOK 1:
The Mystery Monster

BY AMY MARIE
STADELMANN

🪔 ALADDIN
An imprint of Simon & Schuster Children's Publishing Division
1230 Avenue of the Americas, New York, New York 10020
First Aladdin hardcover edition June 2021
Text copyright © 2021 by Amy Marie Stadelmann
Cover illustration copyright © 2021 by Amy Marie Stadelmann
Interior illustrations copyright © 2021 Amy Marie Stadelmann
All rights reserved, including the right of reproduction in whole or in part in any form.
ALADDIN and related logo are registered trademarks of Simon & Schuster, Inc.
For information about special discounts for bulk purchases, please contact Simon & Schuster
Special Sales at 1-866-506-1949 or business@simonandschuster.com.
The Simon & Schuster Speakers Bureau can bring authors to your live event. For more information
or to book an event contact the Simon & Schuster Speakers Bureau at 1-866-248-3049 or visit
our website at www.simonspeakers.com.
Book designed by Tiara Iandiorio
The illustrations for this book were rendered in pencil and digitally colored.
The text of this book was set in Austral Slab.
Manufactured in China 0321 SCP
10 9 8 7 6 5 4 3 2 1
This book has been cataloged with the Library of Congress.
ISBN 978-1-5344-5161-2 (hc)
ISBN 978-1-5344-5160-5 (pbk)
ISBN 978-1-5344-5162-9 (eBook)

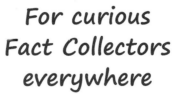

For curious
Fact Collectors
everywhere

Chapter One

In the middle of the city is a strange street where the trees are all twisted. This is Evergreen Street.

ONCE UPON A MOVE

I am the newest resident of this street.
My name is Paige.

ALL ABOUT ME

Name: Paige Turner
Age: 8 years, 3 months, 14 days

favorite color
is yellow

collects facts
in Fact Diary

loves to read
nonfiction

always
double-knots
sneakers

Motto: If you can't prove it, it's not a fact!

I am a Fact Collector. A fact is a true piece of information. When I discover a fact I love, I write it in my Fact Diary.

When arriving in a new place, it is helpful to collect facts to feel at home. So far I have collected several facts about Evergreen Street.

48

3→

25

The street has exactly seventy-three windows.

57

72   73

Every full moon they have a street festival.

DON'T MISS IT!

EVERGREEN'S FULL MOON FESTIVAL!

Hiya!

A boy called Penn lives next door to me.

Name: Penn
Age: 6 months in cat years
(8 human years)

refuses to choose
favorite color

talks a lot!

loves to read
fantasy books

has a pet
cat named
Shazbat

Motto: Anything is possible!

Penn loves to talk almost as much
as I love to collect facts!

Sidewalk dog poop . . .

a kid with a pet rock . . .

My rock's name is Lloyd. He is shy.

17

Chapter Two

I stopped in my tracks.
Did he just say what
I thought he said?

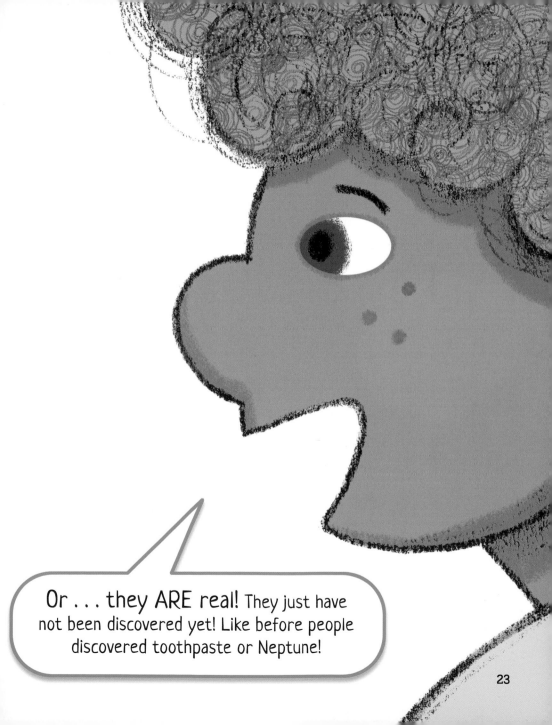

Or . . . they ARE real! They just have not been discovered yet! Like before people discovered toothpaste or Neptune!

It's hard to admit, but Penn makes a good point.

Fact: Neptune is a planet
that was discovered in 1846.

But before that, some very smart people only GUESSED that it was there.

They had to do a lot of tricky math to PROVE their guess was, in fact . . . A FACT!

All facts start off as guesses.

But with evidence, a guess can be proven to be a fact . . . or not.

As Penn is telling me about the undiscovered
monster of Evergreen Street . . . I have an idea!

What if I, Paige the Fact Collector, could prove whether the guess about this monster, was a fact? Then I could write a fact in my Fact Diary, a fact that I had proven myself!

The Very Serious NEWSPAPER

PAIGE PROVES IT!

Real-Life Monster Lives on Evergreen Street.

Exclusive Interview!

The Very Serious NEWSPAPER

PAIGE PROVES IT!

Absolutely No Such Thing as Monsters.

Smartest Kid Alive!

One way or another, I might even be a part of history!

Chapter Three

We need evidence to prove whether the monster is a fact, and evidence needs to be INVESTIGATED. With Penn's help, I make a list.

MONSTER EVIDENCE:

- leaves behind footprints

- hides in the bushes

- scary screeches

That means I need to see these
monster-size footprints for myself.

They are curious footprints.
I do my best to capture the size
and shape in my notebook.

But does this footprint really belong to a monster?

It is too big to be a cat's.

It is too pointy to be a human's.

Sometimes the facts jump right into your lap.

Name: Fizzle the dog
Breed: Scottish deerhound

Owner: Ms. M

43

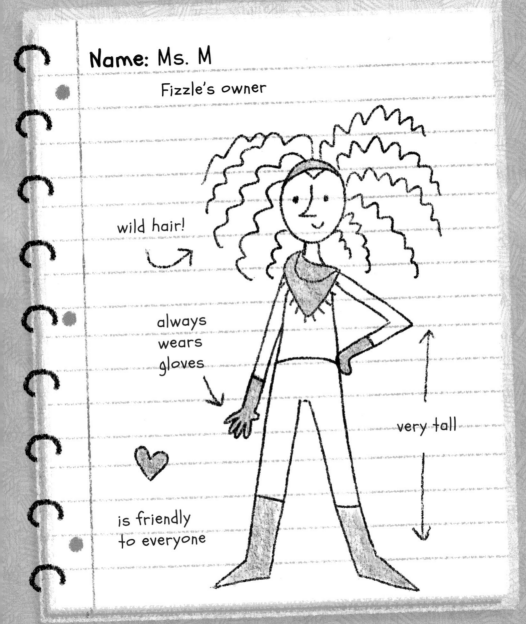

Name: Ms. M

Fizzle's owner

wild hair!

always
wears
gloves

very tall

is friendly
to everyone

45

Ms. M just laughs and gives us a
wink before walking off with Fizzle.

MONSTER EVIDENCE:

~~leaves behind footprints~~

☑ dog paw prints   🐾 Fizzle's!

__ hides in the bushes

__ scary screeches

Chapter Four

Next, Penn and I walk down to the edge of the block.
Penn points at a leafy bush on the corner.

To me, Bryan looks like a normal bush.

But then Bryan starts to shake.

Could a monster really be hiding in the bush?

There is only one way to find out.

I take a deep breath and push aside the leaves. . . .

CHIRP-CHIRP-SQUAWK-CHIRP

Baby birds! A whole nest of them!

53

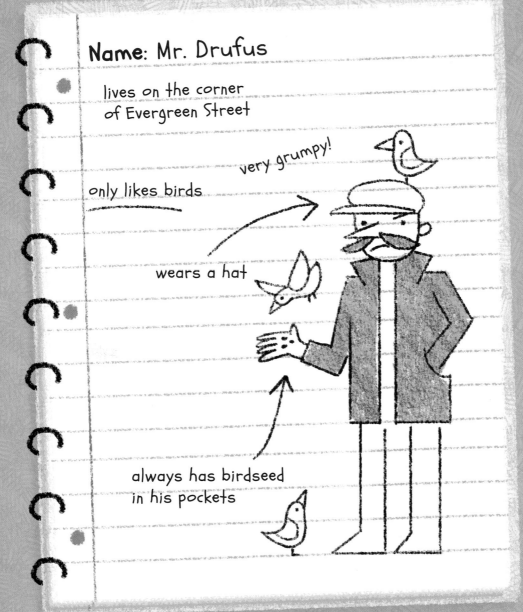

Name: Mr. Drufus

lives on the corner
of Evergreen Street

very grumpy!

only likes birds

wears a hat

always has birdseed
in his pockets

He's not a fan of kids.

MONSTER EVIDENCE:

~~leaves behind footprints~~

☑ dog paw prints 🐾 **Fizzle's!**

~~hides in the bushes~~

☑ bird's nest 🐦 **Baby Birds**

– Scary screeches

So far, none of the evidence has proven there is a monster. But we have one more investigation: scary screeches. Sure enough, when the sun is setting, there is a sudden screeching noise. It is horrible.

Is it someone moving patio furniture?

Or starting up a lawn mower?

Or the creaking of an old rusty gate?

Or could it really be the scary
screeching of a monster?!

But my dad says, "Don't believe everything you hear."
So we had to find out where this noise was coming from.

Was it the mailbox?

Was it the trashcan?

Was it the pet rock?

It looks like a monster!

It sounds like a monster!

But is it?

MONSTER EVIDENCE:

~~leaves behind footprints~~

☑ dog paw prints   Fizzle's!

~~hides in the bushes~~

☑ bird's nest   Baby Birds

~~scary screeches~~

☑ violin   Karla's!

Conclusion:
☑ NO MONSTER

Chapter Six

I have done it!

I, Paige, have proven a fact!

Fact! There is no monster on Evergreen Street. There is a dog, some baby birds, and a bad violin player.

I'm so proud, it's like I can hear music playing!

I had just gotten a cup of hot cocoa when . . .

AROOOO...

ARO

Did you hear that?

Probably Fizzle howling at the full moon. . . .

Or a monster!

There is a strange shadow in the alley!

Chapter Seven

I had to catch my breath for a second.
Now, it's true that some facts are scary.
But scary or not, a fact is always a fact.

Fact: The Earth is struck by lightning 100 times per second.

Fact: The world's largest spider, the giant huntsman, is 12 inches wide— as big as a dinner plate!

It's also a fact that everything looks scarier
in the dark. So maybe what we see is just
Fizzle howling at the moon?

WEREW

A werewolf has two forms, a human form and a wolf form.

In wolf form, werewolves are large beasts covered in thick fur and often have red or yellow eyes.

In human form, appearances vary, but look out for blisters on their hands from walking on all fours.

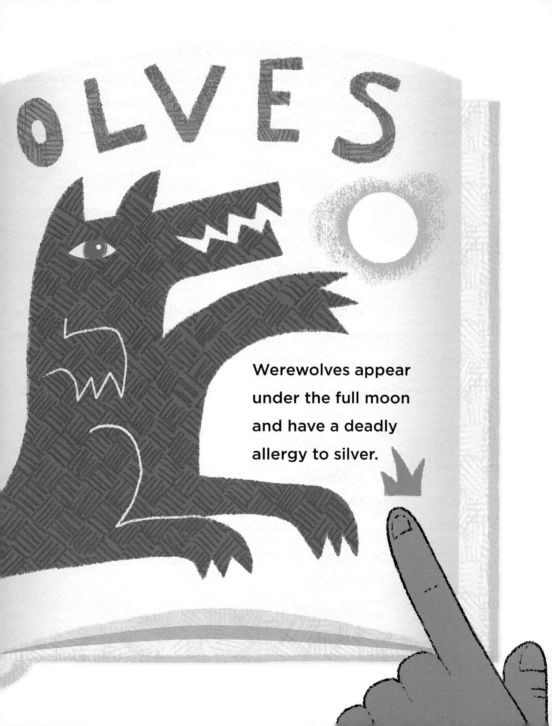

Werewolves appear under the full moon and have a deadly allergy to silver.

After a fact is proven, NEW evidence might show up!

This means facts can change, so you need to prove them again.

And even though Penn's monster book is a book of fiction, could it be pointing to an unproven fact?

Is there a werewolf on Evergreen Street?

Chapter Eight

Fact: a number of humans live on Evergreen Street.

Guess: one of them might be a . . . werewolf!

hiss

What about Mr. Drufus? He's so grumpy!
He could be the werewolf!

NAME: Mr. Drufus
Lives on the corner of Evergreen Street

very grumpy!

wears a hat

only likes birds

Always has bird seed
in his pockets

No. Remember we saw him at the Full Moon Festival complaining about the hot cocoa?

Oh right! Eh, he's too bald to be a werewolf anyway.

What about Karla? She's quiet . . .
maybe she's hiding something?

False. I recall seeing her at the festival, talking to the kid with the pet rock.

Oh shucks. And she's probably too short. . . .

What about Ms. M? I don't remember seeing her at the Full Moon Festival.

But she's so nice!

Who says a werewolf can't be nice?
Also, why do you think she
always wears gloves?

Chapter Nine

One of the best ways to check evidence is to go to the source: That's right, Ms. M.'s house.

Ms. M's home doesn't look like the home of a werewolf. But then again, I've never been to the home of a werewolf . . . that I know of.

I couldn't wait one more second!
I had a question that needed an answer.

Ms. M, can I ask you about your gloves?
Why do you always wear them?

It is time to get to the truth, once and for all.

At first Ms. M didn't say a word.
No one said a word.

But then she told us what really happened.

The fact is that sometimes two different
people look at the exact same facts and. . .

have two different conclusions.

And that is the real mystery!

Is there a werewolf monster on Evergreen Street?

Or a dog that likes to howl at the moon?

To me, the facts are clear.

Penn and I might not agree,

but there is one thing we DO agree on.

Fact: We are friends!

Yes! So, let me tell you about this ghost I saw once. . . .